S0-BVL-278

To my two little cubs, for all the hours spent pootling about ~ S. S.

For my godson Woody ~ F. I.

tiger tales

5 River Road, Suite 128, Wilton, CT 06897
Published in the United States 2022
Originally published in Great Britain 2021
by Little Tiger Press Ltd.
Text by Stephanie Stansbie

ISBN-13: 978-1-68010-281-9
ISBN-10: 1-68010-281-8
Printed in China
LT/2800/0278/0522

2 4 6 8 10 9 7 5 3 1

www.tigertalesbooks.com

Someday

BY
STEPHANIE STANSBIE

ILLUSTRATED BY
FRANCES IVES

tiger tales®

"Mommy Bear, you are so wonderful,"
said a little cub one morning.
"I want to be just like you."

"One day you will be," said the mommy bear.
"Now you're small like a sapling,
but soon you'll be a tree."
"How soon?" asked the little cub.
"Will I be a tree tomorrow?"

"Not tomorrow.
But someday . . . .

"Someday, you'll run through
tall grasses and leap over
rocks as if they were pebbles.

"You'll climb to the top of the trees
where the sweetest berries grow.
And you'll remember the times we
sat together, sharing a berry feast.

"You'll know how to swim through
the rushing waters and chase
the shimmering fish, because of all
the happy hours we've spent
splashing around together.

"You won't fear the dark or
the hooting of the owl.

"And your limbs will be strong
from all of our playful tumbling.

So you'll know how to fall down
and get back up again.

"Someday, you'll meet another bear who's grown. And maybe you'll have fluffy little cubs, all of your own."

"Will I have fun with them like I do with you?" asked the little cub.

"Oh, you will!" said the mommy bear.
"But first we have memories to make,
you and me, before you are all grown up.

"Like the roots of the tree,
your memories will keep you
strong as you grow
and bloom."

"I'm happy being a sapling for now,"
the little cub said.
"As long as I'm with you."

"I'm happy, too,"
said the mommy bear. "Come close,
and let's snuggle up to sleep.

There will be more fun tomorrow,
and all of the wonderful tomorrows
after that."